I0819456

The SIGNERS *of the* CONSTITUTION *of* THE UNITED STATES OF AMERICA

APPLEWOOD BOOKS

Illustrations by Tom Lynch

For a complete list of books
currently available, please visit us
at www.applewoodbooks.com

ISBN 978-1-4290-9532-7

Printed in the USA

Introduction

After eight years of warfare, the American Revolution was won. The fighting ended in 1781 and a treaty of peace was signed with Great Britain in 1783 acknowledging America's independence. In wartime and up to this point, the thirteen states defined their alliance as a "firm league of friendship" in the Articles of Confederation, which served as the first constitution of the United States. The federal government set up by the Articles was weak: the states maintained their independence and sovereignty. Americans were wary of giving their central government too much power. They did not want to overthrow despotic British rule just to create their own homegrown variety.

But lacking sufficient power to collect taxes, regulate foreign or domestic trade, or create and stabilize a standard currency, the government under the Articles was proving entirely inadequate as the nation fell into a postwar depression. The sense of crisis was heightened by Shays' Rebellion in 1786, an armed uprising of Massachusetts farmers who were losing their homes and livelihoods to creditors. This insurrection helped to convince many (including such leading voices as James Madison, Alexander Hamilton, John Jay, and George Washington) of the need to assemble the Constitutional Convention of 1787 to revise the Articles or create a new constitution that could restructure the government.

With the survival of the Union at stake, all of the states except Rhode Island sent delegates, selected by each state's legislature, to the Convention in Philadelphia that May; of seventy-four men elected, fifty-five delegates attended, thirty-nine of whom went on to sign the document that became the supreme law of the land. The delegates were an impressive group of statesmen, including many members of state legislatures, judges, governors, attorneys general, representatives at the

Continental and Confederation Congress, and Revolutionary leaders; these men were largely well educated and from wealthy backgrounds. About half were just in their thirties or forties, but the delegation also had crucial help from experienced political leaders like Benjamin Franklin and Roger Sherman, of Connecticut, the two oldest delegates at eighty-one and sixty-six, respectively.

George Washington was elected to preside over the proceedings, and it was soon decided that merely making changes to the Articles would not work—the Articles needed to be replaced entirely. The delegates had a lot of work ahead of them. For the most part they knew that an effective central government, one with a wide range of enforceable powers, had to replace the weaker Congress of the Articles, but the delegations were divided about how to do so. Two blueprints for a constitution were put forward: first was the Virginia Plan, crafted primarily by James Madison, calling for three branches of government, including a legislature whose two houses would be formed of a number of representatives proportionate to their state's population or wealth. This was countered by the New Jersey Plan, a proposal presented by William Paterson that the smaller states thought would be more fair, in which each state would have an equal number of representatives, regardless of population. Aspects of both would be used to lay out the framework of the new government after proponents of both plans were able to agree to the Connecticut Compromise introduced by Roger Sherman, whereby states would be represented equally in the Senate but proportionately in the House of Representatives.

For four months, throughout a hot and humid summer, the delegates discussed, debated, argued over, and hammered out these matters and a great many other proposals and concerns as they framed and drafted a Constitution, word by word, sentence by sentence, clause by clause, section by section. Smaller committees were formed to navigate various stages of the process, including the Committee of

Detail, whose job it was to translate the accepted proposals into the first draft of the Constitution, and the Committee of Style, which provided the wording for the final Constitution. Details had been attended to, and necessary concessions were made as the delegates collectively framed a newer, stronger government. On September 17, 1787, after some final deliberations, the thirty-nine delegates profiled in this book signed the completed document. They had created a republic.

CONNECTICUT

William Samuel Johnson (1727–1819). The son of Anglican clergyman Samuel Johnson, the younger Johnson graduated from Yale College in 1744, choosing to pursue a legal career rather than follow his father into the clergy. He served in the Connecticut legislature and went on to represent his colony's interests in England between 1768 and 1771; he then served in Connecticut's colonial supreme court. Politically moderate and able to understand both perspectives after his years in England he remained neutral during the Revolution. Johnson wished for a peaceful resolution to the conflict and did not wholeheartedly support the idea of America's independence, but once it was achieved he gladly joined the making of the new nation's government and he served in the Confederation Congress from 1785 to 1787. As a delegate at the Constitutional Convention in 1787, he was a major voice for compromise (indeed, he was the delegate who proposed the Connecticut Compromise formally) and was instrumental in advocating for equal representation of the states in the national legislature. Johnson also acted as the chair of the small Committee of Style, which revised the Constitution and gave it its final form. After ratification, Johnson became one of

Connecticut's first U.S. senators and was later the president of King's College (now Columbia University). He lived to be ninety-two.

ROGER SHERMAN (1721–1793). Born on April 19, 1721, in Newton, Massachusetts, Sherman moved to Connecticut in 1743 and established a successful political and legal career there even though his formal education had been minimal. Rising through a series of judicial and political positions, Sherman served as a judge in the Connecticut Superior Court from 1766 to 1789. At the age of sixty-six he was the second-oldest delegate (after Benjamin Franklin) to attend the Constitutional Convention; he was also one of only two delegates who signed the Declaration of Independence, the Articles of Confederation, and the Constitution. The leader of his state's delegation, he was well respected among all the delegates and played an important and influential role in framing the Constitution: Sherman was instrumental in proposing the Connecticut Compromise, the plan incorporated into the Constitution by which each state has equal representation in the Senate and proportional representation in the House of Representatives. After the ratification of the Constitution, which Sherman had been a strong voice for in his state and throughout New England, he represented Connecticut in the House of Representatives from 1789 to 1791 and in the Senate from 1791 until his death in 1793.

Roger Sherman

DELAWARE

George Read (1733–1798). Born and raised in Cecil County, Maryland, Read moved with his family as an infant to New Castle County, Delaware. He studied law in Philadelphia and was admitted to the Pennsylvania bar in 1753. Read was appointed crown attorney general for the three Delaware counties in 1763 until he left for the Continental Congress in 1774. He was politically conservative and tried to work toward reconciliation with England once the Revolution broke out. When Congress voted on American independence on July 2, 1776, Read voted against it. Despite his initial reservations, he did sign the official Declaration of Independence the following month, the only signatory to have previously voted against independence. During the Constitutional Convention he worked to support the interests of small states, and he also followed Alexander Hamilton in supporting a strong central government. At one point Read took an unusual position, openly advocating for the abolition of the states and arguing for the consolidation of the country under one powerful national government. He was an active proponent for ratifying the Constitution, and he led Delaware to become the first state to do so. From 1789 to 1793, Read represented his state in the U.S. Senate, leaving that position to become chief justice of Delaware.

Gunning Bedford Jr. (1747–1812). Born to a wealthy family in Philadelphia, Bedford attended the

College of New Jersey (now Princeton University) and roomed there with future U.S. president James Madison. He served in the Revolutionary War and in 1776 was promoted to muster-master-general of New York. He is thought to have perhaps served briefly as an aide to General George Washington. After the war he was admitted to the Delaware bar, and entered private practice in Dover, Delaware from 1779 to 1783, the year he became a delegate to the Continental Congress; he also served as attorney general for his state. As a member of the Constitutional Convention, Bedford was an outspoken advocate for small states. After the Constitution was adopted, President Washington appointed Bedford as a federal district judge for Delaware, a position he held until his death in 1812. It was also during his later years that he became an advocate for the abolition of slavery.

John Dickinson (1732–1808). Dickinson, whose father was a tobacco planter and judge, was born in Talbot County, Maryland. While he was still a boy, his family moved to Delaware, where he was educated at home by his parents and excellent private tutors. He went to London in 1753 to study law. Upon his return in 1757, he was admitted to the Pennsylvania bar. Rising in prominence as a lawyer, he entered politics and served in public offices while also gaining recognition for his writing; he authored a number of important pamphlets articulating colonial issues with British governance. As a Pennsylvania delegate to the Continental Congress, in 1775 he composed the "Olive Branch Petition," Congress's last attempt for peace with Britain. He advocated for reconciliation with the Crown, rather than revolution and independence, and left Congress without signing the Declaration of Independence. Still, he helped to draft the Articles of Confederation and served in the Delaware militia. He served as president of Pennsylvania and then Delaware, and the latter state sent him as a delegate to the Constitutional Convention; his background allowed him to understand the perspectives of both small states and large ones. While he supported a strong central government, he wanted to make sure that each state, regardless of size, would have an equal voice in the Senate. It was Dickinson who prepared the early drafts of the First Amendment. Because of an illness, he authorized fellow delegate George Read to sign the Constitution on his behalf. He died in 1808; Dickinson College (he had donated land for its establishment) in Carlisle, Pennsylvania, was named for him and his wife, Mary.

Richard Bassett

RICHARD BASSETT (1745–1815). As a young man, he studied law before being admitted to the bar in Delaware. During the Revolution he served in a Delaware militia as captain of the Dover Light Horse Regiment from 1777 to 1781. After the Revolution he served in the state senate and house before being chosen as a delegate to the Constitutional Convention. Though he was well respected, he was relatively quiet amid the debates of the Convention. He was elected to the U.S. Senate in 1789, where he served until 1793. Bassett was chief justice of the Delaware Court of Common Pleas from 1793 to 1799 and governor of Delaware from 1799 to 1801, before President John Adams just before leaving office (in one of his so-called midnight appointments) made him a judge of the U.S. Circuit Court. Under the new president, Thomas Jefferson, this position was soon abolished and Bassett returned to Maryland, where he was born and lived out his remaining years as a planter.

Jacob Broom (1752–1810). Broom was the son of a prosperous Delaware blacksmith and farmer. After attending Wilmington's Old Academy, he became a successful farmer, surveyor, and local businessman. He held several local political offices before joining the state legislature, where he served for four years before he was chosen to represent Delaware at the Constitutional Convention in 1787; he attended each session of the Convention faithfully but remained mostly in the background. He spoke out several times on a few issues, among them the interests of small states and his reservations about giving too much power to the executive, but for the most part, he left the oratory to others. Another delegate, William Pierce of Georgia, described Broom as "a plain good Man, with some abilities, but nothing to render him conspicuous." Upon his return to Wilmington, he served as the city's first postmaster and then other small political roles as well as pursuing several business enterprises. He later helped his alma mater, Old Academy, reorganize into the College of Wilmington, where he served on the college's first board of trustees until his death.

GEORGIA

WILLIAM FEW (1748–1828). Few was born into a poor farming family in Maryland. They moved to North Carolina in the 1750s, where their situation improved until they became involved with the Regulators, a populist movement against the royal governor. When the protest movement was defeated, Few's brother was hanged for his part in it and the family's farm was destroyed. Now living in Georgia, Few joined the militia in 1775, casting his lot with the Patriot cause. He served too in the state's provincial congress and its assembly, among other political roles, in the late 1770s before his election to the Continental Congress in 1780. He was appointed as a delegate to the Constitutional Convention, though he never spoke during the proceedings, and he did attend the state's ratifying. He was one of Georgia's first senators before moving to Manhattan in 1799 to become president of the City Bank of New York. After sixteen years of public service in New York, Few retired to his country home in Fishkill, New York, where he died in 1828.

ABRAHAM BALDWIN (1754–1807). Baldwin, born in Connecticut, graduated from Yale College in 1772 and was ordained a Congregational minister three years later, serving as a chaplain in the Continental Army during the Revolution. After the war, Baldwin moved to Georgia and joined the state legislature. From this position he helped found Franklin College (later the University of

Georgia) and became its first president. He was a delegate to the Continental Congress and then to the Constitutional Convention, where he helped facilitate the compromise between the small and large states over representation in Congress. He was elected to the U.S. House of Representatives in 1788 and served there until moving to the Senate in 1799, remaining in that house until his death in 1807. He was buried at Rock Creek Cemetery in Washington, D.C.

MARYLAND

James McHenry (1753–1816). McHenry moved from Ireland, the country of his birth, to North America in 1771, having been sent ahead of his family to recuperate from what they saw as his "excessive study habits." He attended Newark Academy in Delaware before settling in Philadelphia, where he apprenticed under Dr. Benjamin Rush before becoming a practicing doctor and surgeon. He served as a surgeon to the Continental Army during the Revolution, was captured in 1776 and held briefly as a prisoner of war, and eventually worked on the staff of General George Washington. He served in the Maryland Senate for five years beginning in 1781; he was also a member of Congress. As a delegate at the Constitutional Convention, he did not participate greatly in the debates or proceedings, but his detailed notes about the events became an important historical source. After strongly supporting ratification he again sat in the state assembly and then senate before, in 1796, being appointed secretary of state by President Washington, a position he continued in under President John Adams. Fort McHenry, built to defend Baltimore Harbor and completed in 1803, was named in his honor.

DANIEL OF ST. THOMAS JENIFER (1723–1790). He was born on an estate near Port Tobacco, Maryland, the son of a wealthy doctor. From a young age he began a lifetime of public service, including a stint as justice of the peace for Charles County, Maryland, where he lived, and as a representative in the upper house of the state senate, among many other offices he held. A supporter of the Patriot cause, during and after the Revolution Jenifer became involved in the new nation's political affairs. At the Constitutional Convention he was, like his good friend Benjamin Franklin, among the oldest delegates and considered one of the elder statesmen present. Jenifer generally shared the positions of James Madison, and his best-known contribution at the Convention was his proposal for three-year terms in the U.S. House of Representatives. Afterward, Jenifer retired to his plantation near Annapolis, Maryland, where he died in 1790.

DANIEL CARROLL (1730–1796). One of the few Roman Catholics among the Founding Fathers, Carroll was educated under the Jesuits at the College of St. Omer in France. He was elected to the state senate and council and served in the Continental Congress before attending the Constitutional Convention, where Carroll advocated for a centralized, strong federal government though he did also believe that some powers not specifically delegated to the central government should fall to the states, or to individuals. He was persuasive campaigning in Maryland for ratification of the document and was afterward elected to the U.S. Senate. In 1791 Carroll was one of three commissioners appointed to survey and acquire land for the newly designated District of Columbia and the new federal capital there. He served on the commission until his resignation due to ill health in 1795. He died a year later at the age of sixty-nine.

MASSACHUSETTS

NATHANIEL GORHAM (1738–1796). He was born in Charlestown, Massachusetts, the son of a sea captain. At fifteen years of age he apprenticed with a merchant in New London, Connecticut, and returned to Charlestown in 1759 to begin his own merchant house. In the 1770s, Gorham served in the colonial legislature and then as delegate to the Massachusetts Provincial Congress, among other roles in state politics; he joined the Continental Congress in 1782. As delegate to the Constitutional Convention, he was elected as presiding officer of the Committee of the Whole, meaning that he, rather than Convention president George Washington, presided over sessions during deliberations. He was active and outspoken, supporting a strong central government. He then worked hard to see that the Constitution was ratified by his state, though he did not join the new government afterward. A large real estate deal he was involved in collapsed, and he was devastated financially. He died in 1796 and was buried in the Phipp Street Cemetery in Charlestown.

RUFUS KING (1755–1827). Born in Maine (then part of Massachusetts), Rufus graduated from Harvard College in 1777. He interrupted his study of law in 1778 to briefly join the militia, and he fought in the Battle of Rhode Island. He then returned to law, was admitted to the bar, and began a legal practice in Newburyport, Massachusetts, in 1780. King was first elected to the Massachusetts legislature in 1783 and the Continental Congress in 1784, becoming one of its youngest members. Though only thirty-two, he was sent to the Constitutional Convention and soon became a leading figure in the deliberations, favoring a strong federal government and supporting the interests of the large northern states. King, a longtime opponent of slavery, spoke out against the institution at the Convention and disliked the three-fifths compromise for southern taxation and representation, whereby an enslaved person was counted as a fraction of a free person. He served as one of the first U.S. senators from New York and at various times ran as a Federalist candidate for vice president and president. He was appointed the minister to Great Britain from 1796 to 1803 and again from 1825 to 1826 before falling ill and dying the following year.

NEW HAMPSHIRE

John Langdon (1741–1819). Langdon, the son of a prosperous shipbuilder, came from one of the first families to settle in Portsmouth, New Hampshire. By age twenty-two he was the captain of his own cargo ship and making regular voyages to the West Indies; he soon had a small fleet and by 1777 was one of the wealthiest men in Portsmouth. He was a strong supporter of the Revolutionary cause from the beginning, and when war broke out he supervised the construction of several American warships and also fought in several battles and helped fund troops for the effort. After the war, he served two terms as the president of New Hampshire before being elected to both the Continental Congress and the Constitutional Convention. Though the New Hampshire delegation arrived late to the Convention, he contributed to the committee that created the compromise on slavery and he worked to strengthen the federal government. He served his state as a U.S. senator before returning to the New Hampshire legislature, then becoming governor of the state from 1805 to 1812, when he retired from public life. He died in Portsmouth in 1819.

Nicholas Gilman (1755–1814). The son of a well-to-do merchant family, Gilman was educated in Exeter, his hometown, before the start of the Revolutionary War, when he enlisted in a local militia unit and served as an assistant adjutant general before rising to the rank of captain; he saw action in many of the war's major battles, including Saratoga, Monmouth, and Yorktown. His military experience helped him to enter politics, and he was appointed to the Continental Congress. As a delegate to the Constitutional Convention in 1787 he played just a small role and did not join the debates; he called the resulting document "the best that could meet the unanimous concurrence of the states in Convention; it was done by bargain and compromise." Still, attending the Convention impressed upon him the great importance of the Constitution, and he was an important advocate for New Hampshire's ratification. Gilman served four terms in the U.S. House of Representatives before holding various state offices and then being elected to the U.S. Senate in 1805, where he served until his death in 1814.

Nicholas Gilman

NEW JERSEY

WILLIAM LIVINGSTON (1723–1790). Born in Albany, New York, Livingston graduated from Yale College in 1741. He went to New York City, was admitted to the bar, and opened a legal practice in 1752. Livingston became active in politics and served in the New York colonial legislature; he also began to gain influence as the author of broadsides, newspaper articles, and verse. Having moved to New Jersey, he represented that state in the Continental Congress between 1774 and 1776, when he assumed a leadership role in the state's militia and later that year became the first governor of New

Wil: Livingston

Jersey. He remained active as governor while serving as a delegate to the Constitutional Convention, but holding both roles may have kept him from playing a larger part in the debates. At sixty-three, he was among the older and the more experienced delegates present, and though he did initially support the New Jersey plan, which would have favored small states, he then worked toward a compromise. He came away from the Convention eager to secure his state's ratification and was active in doing so before resuming his duties as governor, a position he continued to hold until his death.

David Brearley (1745–1790). Brearley studied law at the College of New Jersey (now Princeton University) and went into practice in that field. In the years leading up to the Revolution, Brearly was an outspoken opponent of British taxation. He joined the New Jersey militia in 1776, serving in the Continental Army until 1779; he rose to the rank of captain and participated in the battles of Brandywine, Germantown, and Monmouth. In 1779 he began a ten-year tenure as the chief justice of the New Jersey Supreme Court. At the Constitutional Convention in 1787, Brearley was chairman of the Committee on Postponed Parts, which played an important role in resolving some difficult tabled issues and thus shaping the final version of the Constitution. Afterward, he was appointed by President Washington to the U.S. District Court for New Jersey, though he served for only a year before his death in 1790.

David Brearley.

William Paterson (1745–1806). Born in Ireland, Paterson immigrated to America at age two. Like many fellow delegates, he attended the College of New Jersey (later Princeton University); he studied law and was admitted to the bar in 1768. The following year he founded the college's Cliosophic Society, a political, literary, and debating society, with Aaron Burr. He helped write the constitution of New Jersey in 1776 and served as the state's first attorney general until 1783. At the Constitutional Convention, he introduced and was the main proponent of the New Jersey Plan, which would have kept and expanded a unicameral Congress in which states were equally represented, as under the Articles of Confederation. Proposing and debating this plan helped the smaller states to have their concerns addressed in the compromise that followed. Elected to the U.S. Senate in 1798, Paterson resigned the following year (the first senator ever to do so) to succeed fellow delegate William Livingston as governor of New Jersey. In 1793 President Washington appointed Paterson to the Supreme Court, where he was a justice for thirteen years, until the time of his death.

Jonathan Dayton (1760–1824). Born in Elizabeth, New Jersey, he too attended the College of New Jersey (later Princeton University), graduating in 1776 and serving in the Continental Army as an officer throughout the war. He went on to become a lawyer and a land speculator, also entering politics and serving in the New Jersey legislature. At twenty-six he was the youngest delegate to attend the Constitutional Convention, and he did not play a large role in the debates, though he did help amplify the concerns of the small states. After the convention, Dayton spent eight years in the U.S. House of Representatives, becoming the Speaker of the House, and in 1799 was elected to the U.S. Senate. His national political career ended in 1807 when he was charged with conspiring with Aaron Burr to commit treason in attempting to have western states and territories secede from the United States. This accusation was never proven and did not come to trial, but Dayton afterward held only local and state offices. Because of his vast landholdings in Ohio, the city of Dayton was named after him in 1796.

NEW YORK

Alexander Hamilton (1755 or 1757–1804). Hamilton immigrated to America from the British West Indies to attend King's College (now Columbia University) in 1773, and as a student began to write pro-Whig political pamphlets that were widely read and very influential. He served in the Revolutionary War, for four years as aide-de-camp to General Washington. He served in the Continental Congress and the New York legislature after the Revolution and began to practice law in New York City. At the Constitutional Convention, his support for a strong central government diverged from the opinions of the other two New York delegates (neither of whom went on to sign the Constitution), and many of his views were generally thought too extreme and were not accepted by the others present. Thus he had a limited influence on the proceedings, but he was instrumental in getting the document ratified by New York and accepted more broadly, particularly with *The Federalist*, the essays he wrote with James Madison and John Jay (though he was the primary author) aimed at convincing his state to ratify and well known now as an enduring argument justifying the Constitution and the establishment of a strong federal government. President Washington appointed Hamilton as the first secretary of the treasury in 1789, a position he held until 1795, and he developed the plan for the Bank of the United States, chartered by Congress in 1791. During the election of 1800 Hamilton became bitter enemies with Aaron Burr, who killed him in a duel on July 12, 1804.

NORTH CAROLINA

William Blount (1749–1800). Born to a prominent North Carolina family, he served in the Continental Army as a paymaster and was elected to the state legislature in 1781, serving there and in the Continental Congress in various roles throughout the decade. He did not speak during the Constitutional Convention and was pessimistic about the outcome, arriving late and staying only a short time before returning to Congress. He was wary of signing the final document but did so despite his reservations. In 1790 President Washington appointed Blount the first governor of the Southwest Territory (including Tennessee), created from land ceded by North Carolina to the United States. When Tennessee became a state in 1796, Blount was elected to represent it in the U.S.

Senate. The following year, facing financial problems connected to his land speculations in the West, he concocted an illegal scheme that would have allowed Britain to gain control of Florida and Louisiana from France. His misdeeds discovered, Blount became the first person to be impeached and he was expelled from Congress for his actions. He returned to Tennessee, where, still popular, he was elected to the state senate in 1798, two years before his death.

RICHARD DOBBS SPAIGHT (1758–1802). Born in North Carolina, he was orphaned at eight and sent to be educated in Ireland. After attending the University of Glasgow, Spaight returned in 1778, where he fought in the Revolution in a regiment of a North Carolina militia. He was then elected to the state legislature, serving in the Continental Congress between terms, from 1782 to 1785, before attending the Constitutional Convention. At twenty-nine he was one of the youngest delegates to sign the Constitution, and though he did not make major contributions while at the Convention, he believed in a strong federal government, was present at every session, and advocated for his state to ratify afterward. He retired from politics for a time due to ill health but in 1792 was elected governor of North Carolina, in which office he served three terms. He was elected to the U.S. House of Representatives in 1798 but served just one term before losing his 1800 reelection bid to John Stanly; he returned to his state legislature for a year or so. In 1802, at age forty-four, Spaight was mortally wounded in a duel with Stanly, the political rival who had taken his seat in Congress.

Hugh Williamson (1735–1819). Williamson was born in southeastern Pennsylvania to parents who had emigrated from Ireland and ran a clothier business; he graduated from the College of Philadelphia (later the University of Pennsylvania) in 1757. Pursuing his talents in many fields, he trained in theology and attained a master's degree in mathematics before studying in Europe, where he earned his medical degree in 1764. Williamson, who was witness to the Boston Tea Party in 1773, then settled in North Carolina and served with some renown in its militia as surgeon general during the Revolution. Following the war, he was elected to the state legislature and the Continental Congress. As a delegate to the Constitutional Convention, he was a champion of Federalism and gave many speeches, a member also of five committees. He worked hard for North Carolina's ratification and was elected from his state to the U.S. House of Representatives afterward, serving two terms. In 1793 he moved to New York and continued his academic and scientific pursuits; he died and was buried there in 1819.

PENNSYLVANIA

Benjamin Franklin (1705–179). Franklin, one of seventeen children, was born in Boston. With little formal education, he primarily educated himself. He started his career at an early age, becoming a printer and writer based in Philadelphia whose work, especially *Poor Richard's Almanac*, was soon known throughout the colonies. By the time he entered the Pennsylvania legislature, in 1751, the multitalented Franklin had also already found success with his scientific experiments and inventions. Beginning in 1757 he spent much of his time in England, representing the interests of Pennsylvania and other colonies, returning home in 1775 and helping to draft the Declaration of Independence, which he also signed. Franklin proved to be an extraordinary diplomat when he went to France in 1776, securing that nation's military and economic assistance for the American Revolution; he also played a vital role in negotiating the final peace treaty with the British in 1783. With these substantial accomplishments behind him, at eighty-one Franklin was the oldest delegate at the Constitutional Convention in Philadelphia that summer and was quite well known already. His position at the Convention was more honorary than official, and he rarely engaged in debate, though he helped to keep a focus on the republican principles of the new nation and to work out compromises. Among the Founding Fathers, only he signed all four of the Declaration, the Treaty of Alliance with France, the Treaty of Paris (which ended the war), and the Constitution, which could be said to be the documents that created the United States. He was in poor health during the Convention and was rarely seen in public afterward. He died of pleurisy at his home in Philadelphia on April 17, 1790, eighty-four years old.

THOMAS MIFFLIN (1744–1800). Born and raised in Philadelphia, Mifflin, the son of Quaker parents, graduated from the College of Philadelphia (now the University of Pennsylvania) in 1760. He was elected in

1772 to the Pennsylvania legislature, where he joined the colonial opposition to British policies and served for four years; also during this time he attended the Continental Congress. During the Revolution he acted as an aide-de-camp to General Washington and then as the first quartermaster general to the Continental Army, rising to the rank of major general by 1777, though allegations that he had conspired against Washington led him to resign. Still, when the war ended he served two terms representing his state in the Confederation Congress and in 1783 was president of that body. He was speaker of the Pennsylvania assembly beginning in 1785, and went from there to the Constitutional Convention, though he did not speak or serve on committees. Mifflin returned to the state legislature and chaired the committee that wrote the state's constitution. He succeeded Benjamin Franklin as president of Pennsylvania, and was elected in 1790 as the state's first governor, a position he held until 1799. He died in Lancaster, Pennsylvania, on January 23, 1800.

Robert Morris (1734–1806). English born, Morris came to America as a teenager, rising to become a successful merchant and serve in Pennsylvania's legislature. He came around to the Revolutionary position more slowly than others, initially voting against independence at the Continental Congress in 1776 before he relented and signed the Declaration. As congressman, Morris procured weapons and other provisions for the Revolutionary armies during the war, a vital service, but in doing so engaged in much self-dealing for his own profit, adding to his great wealth. Asked by George Washington to become superintendent of finance in 1781, Morris turned the Confederation around from the brink of insolvency at a crucial moment, even drawing on his own personal funds, among other sources, to make the Yorktown campaign possible; for this role he became known as the Financier of the Revolution. He returned to the Pennsylvania legislature in 1785 and was a delegate to the Constitutional Convention in 1787, where he was rarely involved in the debates and did not sit on a committee. He believed in a strong central government and was instrumental, however, in getting Pennsylvania to ratify the document. Morris turned down the appointment to be first secretary of the treasury from President Washington, suggesting Alexander Hamilton for the position instead, and joined the U.S. Senate from 1789 to 1795. During that time, his land speculations led him into debt; unable to pay his creditors, he was arrested in 1798 and spent three years in debtor's prison. Afterward, still impoverished, he lived humbly until his death in 1806.

George Clymer (1739–1813). Orphaned as an infant, Clymer was raised in Philadelphia by an aunt and uncle and trained to be a merchant. A leader in the Patriot cause in Philadelphia, he was elected to the Continental Congress in 1776, serving until the next year and also between 1780 and 1782. He was also chosen to represent his state as a signatory of the Declaration of Independence. Clymer joined the Pennsylvania legislature in 1785, which led to his being chosen as a delegate to the Constitutional Convention, where he made some small contributions to the debates and served on committees. He was elected to the U.S. House of Representatives in 1789 and did not seek a second term, instead fulfilling appointments from President Washington as a tax collector and then negotiator of a treaty with the Creek Indians. Afterward, he remained active in civic and philanthropic affairs, becoming the first president of both the Philadelphia Bank and the Pennsylvania Academy of Fine Arts, among other such posts Clymer held before his death in 1813. He was buried at the Friends Burying Ground in Trenton, New Jersey.

THOMAS FITZSIMONS (1741–1811). Born in Ireland, FitzSimons settled in Philadelphia at age nineteen, in 1760. He began working as a clerk in a mercantile house and soon formed a successful partnership with his brother-in-law, specializing in the West India trade. Hit heavily by British taxation in the 1760s, FitzSimons was outspoken in his support for the Patriot cause. During the Revolution he commanded a battalion, leaving active duty to serve on a board overseeing the creation of the Pennsylvania navy and to devise defense strategies for the region; he also helped provision American and French forces. At the Constitutional Convention he focused on financial and mercantile issues, believing a strong federal government was needed to regulate and support commerce. FitzSimons was one of just two Roman Catholic signers of the Constitution; afterward he served three terms in the U.S. House of Representatives, aligning himself with Alexander Hamilton's positions. After leaving office he remained active in civic and philanthropic affairs until the time of his death.

Jared Ingersoll

JARED INGERSOLL (1749–1822). Ingersoll was born in New Haven, Connecticut, and upon his graduation from Yale began a legal career in Philadelphia. He went to Europe in 1773 to study further, and when he returned in 1778, he no longer shared his father's Loyalist views and now supported American independence. Ingersoll represented Pennsylvania at the Continental Congress in 1780 and then as delegate to the Constitutional Convention, where he prepared but never delivered a speech that would have advocated leaving significant powers to the states; leaving this opinion unspoken, he rarely participated in any of the debates. He resumed his law practice after the Convention, arguing some cases before the Supreme Court, and also held positions as attorney general of Pennsylvania, U.S. district attorney for the state, and judge of the Philadelphia district court, among other public offices. In the election of 1812, Ingersoll was the Federalist vice presidential candidate on the ticket headed by DeWitt Clinton (they lost to James Madison and Elbridge Gerry).

JAMES WILSON (1742–1798). Wilson, who was very well educated, immigrated from Scotland in 1765 to teach at the College of Philadelphia. After a year, he left the position to study law, and entering practice he soon became a preeminent lawyer. Also a rising political leader, Wilson wrote an influential pamphlet in 1774 arguing that Parliament lacked authority over the colonies and proposing an independent America; the following year he was elected to the Continental Congress. He was among the delegates to the 1787 Constitutional Convention who had the greatest influence in the deliberations, and he served on the powerful Committee of Detail, which produced the first draft of the Constitution. Wilson, a strong believer in democracy, argued for the people to elect the president and the members of Congress directly; he then framed the plan for an electoral college. President Washington named him as one of the six original justices of the Supreme Court in 1789. Like several other fellow delegates, Wilson made unwise land speculations that led him to financial ruin in 1797, and he had to move to New Jersey to avoid being sent to debtor's prison. Even the threat of impeachment was raised, and under this tremendous financial and political stress, he died in August 1798, becoming the first Supreme Court justice to die while on the bench.

James Wilson

Gouverneur Morris (1752–1816). Born into a wealthy family in New York, Morris studied law at King's College (now Columbia University). He was elected to New York's provincial congress in 1775 and served in a militia in 1776, despite having lost a leg in an earlier accident. That year too he helped to draft his state's first constitution. Elected to the Continental Congress in 1778, he was a signer of the Articles of Confederation. After losing reelection the next year, he moved from New York to Philadelphia and practiced law; then

Gouv Morris

he became the assistant superintendent of finance under Robert Morris, later a fellow delegate. At the Constitutional Convention (as delegate from Pennsylvania, his new home) he gave more speeches (173 in total) than any other delegate and advocated for a strong national government; also an ardent abolitionist, he opposed any constitutional protection for slavery, though he was defeated in this battle by the three-fifths clause. As a member of the Committee of Style, Morris was the primary author of the Preamble and significant in giving the Constitution its actual literary form. After the Convention, he served for two years as minister to France, spent several years abroad, and returned to fill an interim position as senator from New York from 1800 to 1803; later he chaired the Erie Canal Commission before his death in 1816.

SOUTH CAROLINA

John Rutledge (1739–1800). Born and raised in Charleston, South Carolina, Rutledge studied law at Middle Temple in England, where he was admitted to the bar in 1760, returning home soon after to practice law. Successful as an attorney, he was also elected to the South Carolina legislature in 1761 and to the Continental Congress in 1774. Rutledge helped draft South Carolina's state constitution and became the state's first president, and then its governor, a position he held until 1782, when he joined the state legislature. At the Constitutional Convention he was among the most influential delegates and served on five committees, including chairing the Committee of Detail. He was a moderate proponent of states' rights and advocated for southern interests; he also held the position that only property owners should be able to serve in any office in the new government. A slaveholder, he fought vigorously against any restrictions on the slave trade. Still, once compromises were reached, he supported the Constitution in its finished form and worked hard for its ratification. In 1789 President Washington appointed Rutledge as one of the five associate justices on the Supreme Court; he served until 1791, when he resigned to become chief justice of the South Carolina Supreme Court. When Washington attempted to appoint him chief justice of the U.S. Supreme Court in 1794, the Senate would not confirm him. He withdrew from public life in 1795 and died in Charleston in 1800.

Charles Cotesworth Pinckney (1746–1825). Born into a family of aristocratic South Carolinian planters, he studied law at Middle Temple in London and was admitted to the bar in England before returning to South Carolina, where he was elected to the provincial assembly in 1770. Pinckney served in the Continental army during the Revolution, rising to the rank of colonel by 1776 and serving as aide-de-camp to General Washington. He served too during this period in the state legislature and senate before he was captured in 1780 during the siege of Charleston (it was Pinckney who had insisted the city be defended at all costs, a poor tactical decision). He was a prisoner of war for two years and, upon his release, was commissioned a brevet brigadier general. After the war, he became one of the most acclaimed attorneys and legislators in South Carolina. As a delegate to the Constitutional Convention, Pinckney believed in a strong central government and defended the interests of the southern elite, arguing that slavery was to the economic benefit of the North as well as the South and that the population of enslaved people should be counted fully toward the basis for congressional representation. He did agree to the abolition of the slave trade in 1808, though he opposed total emancipation. For the most part he retired from public life in 1796, but he was twice the Federalist presidential candidate, in 1804 and 1808, losing both elections. He returned to managing his plantations and lucrative legal practice until his death.

Pierce Butler (1744–1822). Born in Ireland, Butler served in the British army before marrying into a South Carolina family and becoming a wealthy rice planter. Butler was elected to the South Carolina assembly in 1778, also serving in the state's militia during the Revolution before going on to represent the state in the Continental Congress and at the Constitutional Convention. While he was a nationalist who supported a strong union, he also looked out for his state's "special interests," that is, slavery, and defended the institution for political as well as personal reasons; he was one of the largest slaveholders in America. He introduced the fugitive slave provision during the debates, establishing in the Constitution a protection for slavery, which Butler considered a cornerstone of the southern economy. He was later elected to three terms in the U.S. Senate. At the time of his death in 1822 he was one of the wealthiest men in the United States.

Charles Pinckney (1757–1824). Cousin to fellow signer Charles Cotesworth Pinckney, Charles Pinckney came from a wealthy Charleston family. Pinckney studied law and served as a delegate to the Continental Congress in 1777 before beginning to practice law in Charleston. Enlisting as a soldier, Pinckney rose to lieutenant and served at both the siege of Savannah in 1779 and the fall of Charleston in 1780, which led to his capture and a year spent as a prisoner of war. When his father, a prominent lawyer and planter, died in 1782, Pinckney inherited Snee Farm, his family's plantation, along with the enslaved people who worked there. In 1784 he was elected to the Confederation Congress; he also served several terms as a member of the state legislature. During negotiations with Spain, Pinckney was an important advocate for securing navigation rights to the Mississippi River. Pinckney, a nationalist, had critiqued the Articles of Confederation and was chosen to be a delegate at the Constitutional Convention. Pinckney brought many ideas to the Convention and outlined them in his Pinckney Plan, and though historians have disputed how influential he really was, he did contribute to the Constitution in many ways, among them the inclusion of habeas corpus. Following the Convention, Pinckney was elected as governor of South Carolina (he eventually served four terms) and chaired the state constitutional convention in 1790. Pinckney joined the U.S. Senate in 1798 and served as Thomas Jefferson's campaign manager in South Carolina for the 1800 presidential election. Upon his election, Jefferson appointed him minister to Spain. After serving abroad, Pinckney was elected to the House of Representatives, where he advocated against the Missouri Compromise and for the expansion of slavery. Pinckney retired in 1821 and died in 1824.

Charles Pinckney

George Washington (1732–1799). Washington, the son of a wealthy Virginia planter, trained as a surveyor before serving as a colonel in the French and Indian War and later as commander of the forces of Virginia, the highest American military rank at the time. He was a member of the House of Burgesses, where he supported colonial interests against the British, and then of the Continental Congress, which appointed him commander in chief of the Continental Army in 1775. Washington led the army for the duration of the war, overcoming many obstacles to achieve the victory, a reflection of the strength of his character rather than his skill as a military tactician. After the Revolution, Washington returned to Mount Vernon, his farm and home, describing himself in a letter as "retired from all public employments...and able to...tread the paths of private life with heartfelt satisfaction." However, he knew that the powers of Congress would need to be increased from what was given in the Articles of Confederation and that a stronger union was necessary for the success of the new nation. When the call was made for a Convention, Washington was eventually convinced by James Madison and others to become a delegate. Once the delegates convened in Philadelphia, Benjamin Franklin nominated Washington to preside over the proceedings, and he was unanimously elected to do so. Though he did not speak often at the Convention, his presence was enormously influential, and the trust that everyone had in him allowed the delegates to feel comfortable giving more power to the centralized government's chief executive—very much expected to be Washington—than they might have allocated to that office merely in the abstract. After ratification, he was unanimously elected to be president of the new nation; he served two terms (and declined a third), always mindful of avoiding partisanship and setting the tone and precedents for the future of the presidency.

John Blair (1732–1800). The child of a prominent Virginia family, Blair graduated from the College of William and Mary and studied law at Middle Temple, in London. He began his public life in the Virginia House of Burgesses; once the Revolution began, Blair served on several committees in the Virginia legislature, helping to draft the state's constitution. In 1777, Blair was elected as a judge of the general court before becoming the state's chief justice. At the Constitutional Convention, Blair did not speak or serve on a committee, but he supported the positions generally of the Virginia delegation and he helped afterward to secure his state's ratification. In 1789 President Washington nominated Blair as associate justice of the Supreme Court, where he served until resigning in 1796, spending a few quiet years in retirement in Williamsburg until his death in 1800 at the age of sixty-eight.

James Madison (1751–1836). Madison was born into one of the wealthiest landowning families in Virginia, and as a student at the College of New Jersey (now Princeton) he developed a keen interest in political theory and law. Though his health was too poor for active military service, he was an early advocate for American independence and he made his mark in state and local politics beginning in 1776, including his role on the committee that drafted Virginia's constitution and bill of rights. Already well respected as an effective legislator, at the Continental Congress Madison's reputation as a masterful statesman grew. He was a leading voice for reforming the Articles of Confederation, pointing out its failings in his writings, and in 1787 he was the chief proponent and organizer of the Constitutional Convention, for which he prepared rigorously. Widely agreed to have been the most important framer of the Constitution, Madison spoke more than one hundred and fifty times during the proceedings, with one delegate noting that Madison "took the lead in the Convention" and was the "best informed man of any point in debate." Madison argued for the vital importance of a strong federal government, with a system of checks and balances between the branches of the government. Many aspects of the Virginia Plan he shaped with his state's other delegates were adopted, though Madison had to make a number of compromises, including on proportional representation and limiting federal power to veto state laws. To help secure ratification, Madison contributed about one-third of the essays in *The Federalist*, explaining and defending the Constitution and its republican principles. Madison joined the U.S. House of Representatives in 1789, where he drafted and debated Bill of Rights amendments. He served as secretary of state under Thomas Jefferson, then succeeded him in 1809 to become the fourth president of the United States. Madison was the last surviving signer of the Constitution before his death in 1836, at age eighty-five.